to
Robinson

my
wild
cat

Isabelle Simler

Eerdmans Books for Young Readers

Grand Rapids, Michigan

My cat is a wild animal.*

* Just like lions, tigers, and jaguars, domestic cats belong to the feline family.

He is a fierce carnivore*

* *Felis silvestris catus.*

who hunts for his survival.*

* Cats tear their prey using powerful muscles attached to their skulls.

When he runs*

* Cats can run at speeds up to 30 miles per hour.

his athletic body propels him.*

* A cat can run 100 meters in only 9 seconds—faster than any human on record.

He is flexible and elastic.*

* A cat's muscles can shorten or stretch depending on the circumstances.

Nothing escapes this vigilant observer.*

* Cats have a total field of vision that is 287 degrees wide.

During the day, he sees colors in pastel tones.*

* Cats can see yellow and blue, and they don't distinguish green from red.

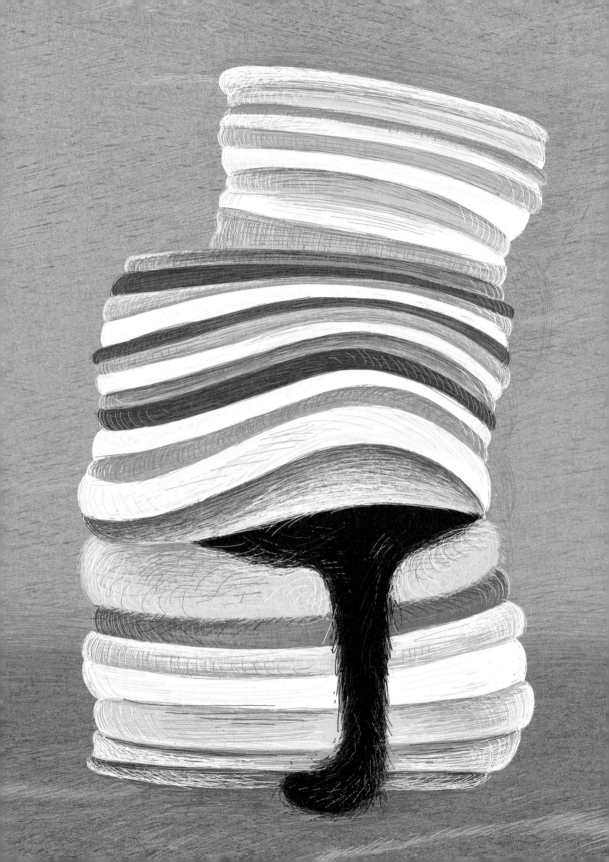

At night he is ruthless, on the lookout.*

* Cats have pupils that dilate and retinas that act as mirrors to reflect light.
Like spies with night vision, they can see well in the dark.

He is agile and acrobatic.*

* A cat's flexible spine and system of balance allow it to land on its feet.

He doesn't hesitate to jump into the water

and to fish for food.

In case of danger,

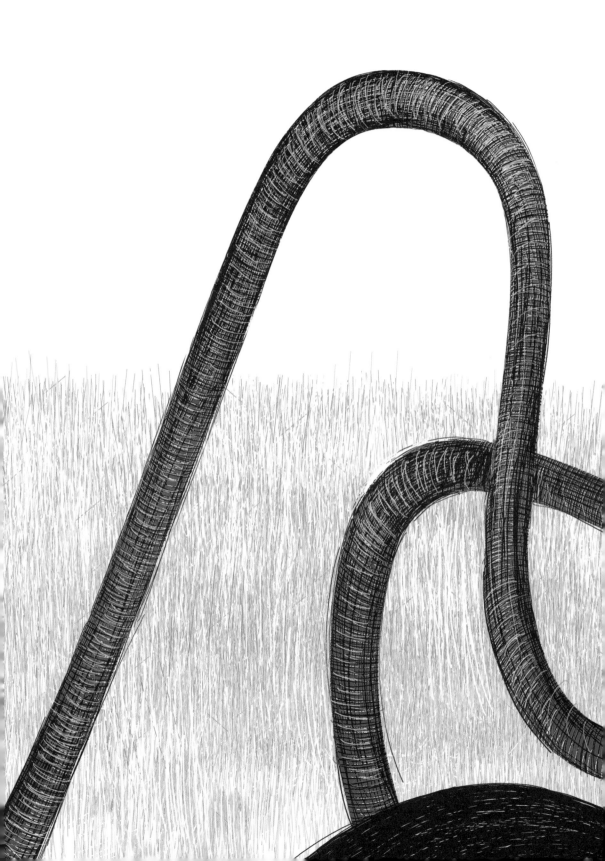

he can disappear

for a long time.

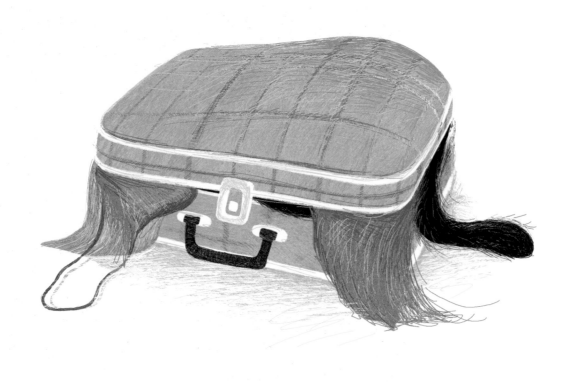

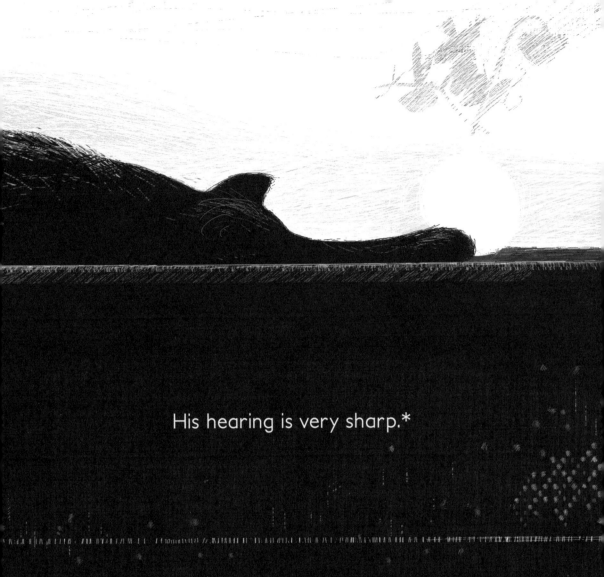

His hearing is very sharp.*

* A cat can hear two octaves more than humans. Each ear has twenty-seven muscles, which allow that ear to move independently to accurately locate the source and distance of a sound.

His sense of smell is very keen.*

* A cat's nasal cavity is filled with hundreds of millions of scent receptors.

His sharp claws sometimes come out by surprise*

* Cats have five claws on each front paw, four on each back paw.
These retractable keratin hooks are wonderful little weapons
hidden in a velvet holster.

but his footsteps are always quiet.*

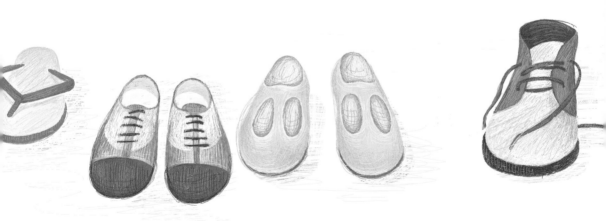

* Cats are digitigrade—they move silently on the tips of their toes. Mechanical
receptors in their paws pick up even the slightest vibration.

At times, my fierce hunter goes on the attack.*

* From the tips of its whiskers to the bottom of its chin, a cat is very sensitive to vibrations, which allows it to detect changes in air pressure and sense when obstacles are nearby.

Then the approach maneuvers begin

and the attempts at camouflage.

His observation post chosen,

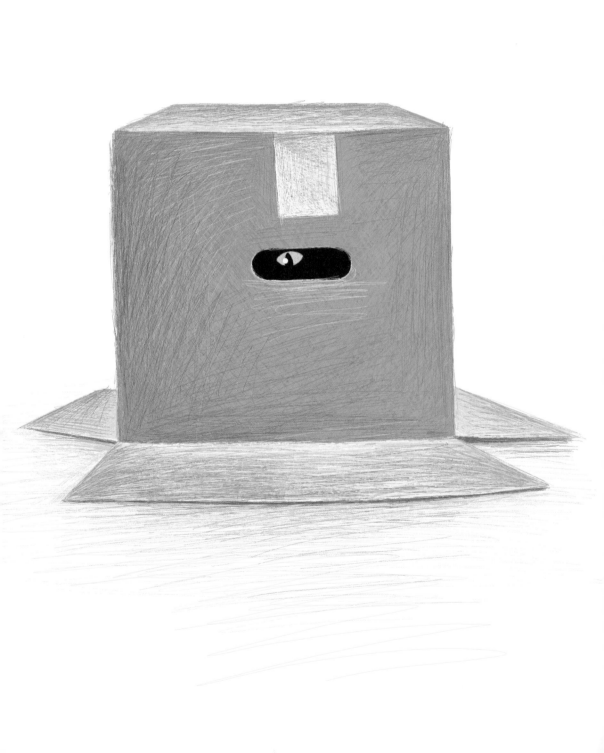

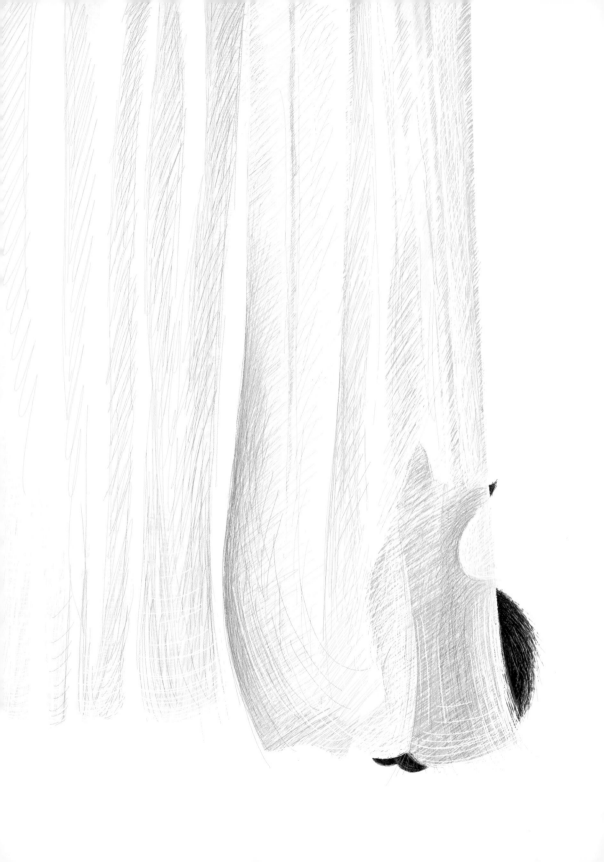

he knows how to be patient

. . .

very patient.

But he always ends up catching his prey

and he takes me down with a single leap.

Isabelle Simler is the award-winning author and illustrator of *The Blue Hour*, *Plume*, and *Sweet Dreamers* (all Eerdmans). Her books have been featured in the Society of Illustrators "The Original Art" Annual Exhibition, and *Plume* was named a 2017 New York Times Best Illustrated Children's Book. Isabelle lives in France. Visit her website at www.isabellesimler.com.

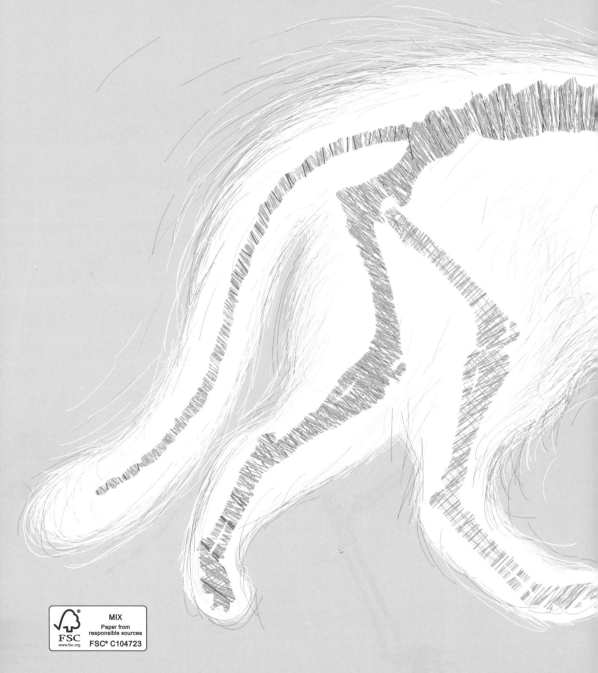

First published in the United States in 2019 by Eerdmans Books for Young Readers, an imprint of Wm. B. Eerdmans Publishing Co. • Grand Rapids, Michigan
www.eerdmans.com/youngreaders • Originally published in France under the title *Mon chat sauvage* by Éditions Courtes et Longues, Paris